FOOTBALL FRIGHTMARE

Steve Barlow and Steve Skidmore

Illustrated by Alex Lopez

EDGE FRANKLIN WATTS

LONDON·SYDNEY

Franklin Watts
First published in Great Britain in 2016 by The Watts Publishing Group

Credits
Series Editor: Adrian Cole
Design Manager: Peter Scoulding
Cover Designer: Cathryn Gilbert
Illustrations: Alex Lopez

HB ISBN 978 1 4451 4384 2
PB ISBN 978 1 4451 4386 6
Library ebook ISBN 978 1 4451 4385 9

Printed in China.

MIX
Paper from
responsible sources
FSC® C104740
FSC
www.fsc.org

Franklin Watts
An imprint of
Hachette Children's Group
Part of The Watts Publishing Group
Carmelite House
50 Victoria Embankment
London EC4Y 0DZ

An Hachette UK Company
www.hachette.co.uk

www.franklinwatts.co.uk

Lin.

Danny.

Sam.

7

"You need to exercise," said Lin.

"Why?" asked Danny.

"So you will live longer," said Lin.

Sam looked puzzled. "Too late —
I'm already undead."

Danny stared at Lin. "We know why you like football. Dogs like chasing balls."

"Are you saying I'm a dog?" asked Lin.

"Er, no," said Danny, quickly.

"Good," said Lin. "Get your football kit and let's go!"

"So who are we playing?" asked Lin.

Jack pointed over at the other team.

Danny and Sam stared in horror.

"Oh, no," said Sam. "It can't be him!"

"It is," groaned Danny.

I am Sam
I am Danny
I am Lin

"I'm not scared of him," said Lin.

"I am," said Danny.

"And me," agreed Sam.

"Don't worry. It will be OK," said Lin.

21

Finally the football match ended.

"13—0 wasn't too bad," said Lin.

"At least I still have both of my legs!" said Sam.

Clogger and his mates left. "Goodbye, losers. I hope you're not too sore," he said.

Lin stared. "Clogger scared everyone off the pitch. He hurt Beth and Jack. Let's give him a scare."

That night Clogger was walking home.

He heard a noise.

He stopped.

"Who's there?" he asked.

Danny, Lin and Sam turned back into human form.

"Are you OK, Clogger? What's wrong?" asked Danny.

Clogger gulped. "I saw a werewolf, a demon and a zombie."

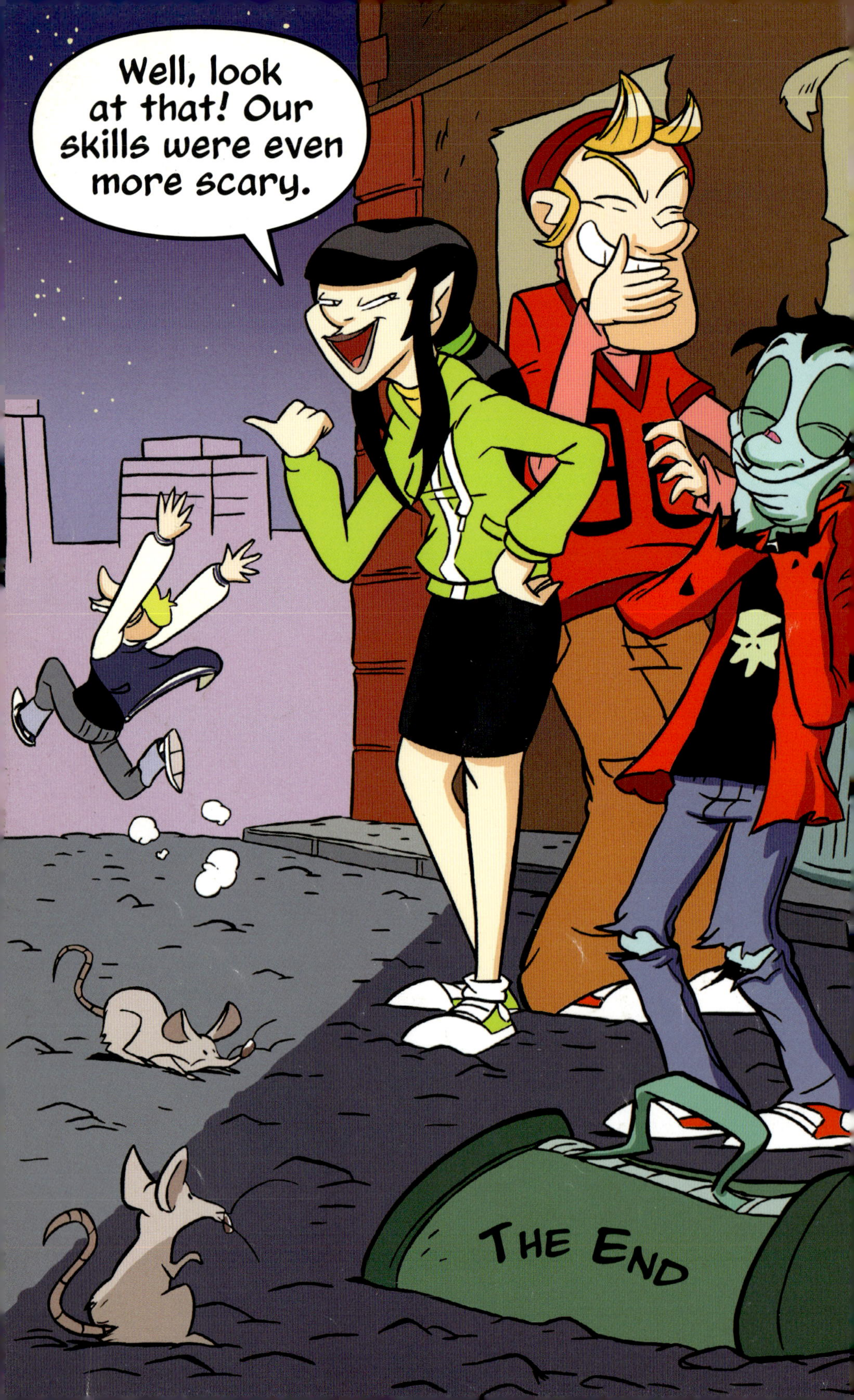
Well, look at that! Our skills were even more scary.
THE END